Poppy Love

Poppy Love titles

Poppy Love Steps Out

Poppy Love Faces the Music

Poppy Love Rock 'n' Roll

Poppy Love Star Turn

Poppy Love In the Spotlight

Poppy Love Tango Queen

Poppy Love Goes for Gold

Visit Poppy Love at
www.poppylovelovestodance.com

Poppy Love
Goes for Gold

NATASHA MAY

illustrated by

SHELAGH McNICHOLAS

WALKER
BOOKS

*With thanks to Neil Kelly and the students of
Rubies Dance Centre
N.M.*

*With thanks to Carolyn, Julia, Kirsty and Ann at
Bell's Dance Centre
S.M.*

First published 2010 by Walker Books Ltd
87 Vauxhall Walk, London SE11 5HJ

2 4 6 8 10 9 7 5 3 1

Text © 2010 Veronica Bennett
Illustrations © 2010 Shelagh McNicholas

The author and illustrator have asserted their moral rights
in accordance with the Copyright, Designs and Patents Act 1988

This book has been typeset in ITC Giovanni

Printed and bound in Great Britain by Clays Ltd, St Ives plc

All rights reserved. No part of this book may be reproduced,
transmitted or stored in an information retrieval system in any form
or by any means, graphic, electronic or mechanical, including
photocopying, taping and recording, without prior written
permission from the publisher.

British Library Cataloguing in Publication Data:
a catalogue record for this book is available from the British Library

ISBN 978-1-4063-2012-1

www.walker.co.uk

Contents

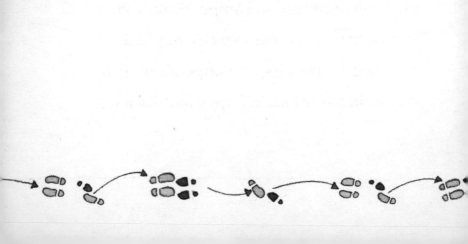

Unlucky Lucky

Poppy Love loved ballroom dancing.

She and her partner, Zack Bishop, had dancing lessons every week with Miss Johnson at the Blue Horizon Dance Studio. They had passed medal tests, and lately they had done well in competitions, too. In fact, they had done so well, they had qualified for the biggest competition of all, the Nationwide Finals. Poppy and Zack were getting more and more excited as the big day came nearer and nearer.

"How many more weeks now?" Zack asked Miss Johnson one Saturday, when the Competition Class children were having an extra lesson. They had been practising the jive and the cha-cha-cha, both energetic dances, and they had just stopped for a break.

"Let me see…" said Miss Johnson. She traced a line on the calendar with her finger. "It will be the first weekend of the Easter holidays, so that's seven weeks."

"Seven weeks!" exclaimed Sam, who would also be competing in the Finals with his partner, Sophie. "It'll feel like seven *years*!"

"No it won't," said curly-haired Cora. "We'll be so busy practising, and getting our costumes ready, the time will fly by."

"And we've still got to go to school," added Luke, Cora's partner. He took a sip from his water bottle. "And I'm in a football tournament too."

"Better make sure you don't get injured playing football, Luke," said Miss Johnson. "We need you in perfect condition at Blackpool!"

Blackpool was the place the Nationwide Finals were being held. It was a seaside resort, just like Brighton, where Poppy and her friends lived. Blackpool was famously the centre of dance festivals, where dancers from all over the world, adults and children, gathered for their most important competitions.

Poppy agreed with Cora. They had so much to do, the time before the Blackpool weekend would go very quickly. Her new dress wasn't even finished yet. "What dress are you taking to Blackpool?" she asked Sophie.

"I'm having a new one," said Sophie. "My mum says the colour's called buttercup yellow."

"Buttercup!" called Sam loudly. "That's a good name for you, Soph, with your yellow hair."

"Don't you start," warned Sophie, who was used to Sam's teasing.

Poppy was just about to tell Sophie about *her* new dress, which was pink, when Miss Johnson clapped her hands for class to begin again. Zack took Poppy's hand. "Back to the cha-cha-cha," he said. "And no slouching!"

Miss Johnson heard him, and smiled. "Quite right," she said. "Slouching won't win any medals at Blackpool or anywhere else. Ready?" She started the cha-cha-cha music. "And *one*, two, that's right, Cora, very nice."

As the children cha-cha-cha'd Miss Johnson went round the class, praising or correcting their movements. She always shared the few boys out as best she could, but every girl had to learn the boy's steps and dance with each other sometimes. Several children in the Competition Class had qualified to take part in the Blackpool Finals, including Emma, who was a good dancer but didn't have a competition partner.

Poppy wished a nice boy who danced as well as Emma would come along to be her partner. But she knew a boy like that would be hard to find. She looked at Emma, who was dancing  with Rosie, a girl of about her height. The girls were a little bit older than Poppy, which made boys even harder to find. Boys of that age were usually more interested in cars, football and computers than dancing.

"Do you think you'll ever give up dancing?" Poppy asked Zack as they danced.

"Not until you do," said Zack.

"Never, then!" cried Poppy.

"Never!" agreed Zack. "Now, stop talking to me. I can't do two things at once."

Miss Johnson was very pleased with the class. At the end of the lesson she stood at the front and applauded, and the children applauded each other, just like in competitions. "If you go on like this for the next seven weeks," said Miss Johnson, "the Blue Horizon Dance Studio might bring more home from Blackpool than a stick of rock!"

"She means we might win something," said Luke on the way out.

"I'd rather have the stick of rock," said Sam, but Poppy knew he was joking.

Neither Mrs Bishop's nor Poppy's mum's car was outside. For a moment Poppy was puzzled, and then she remembered. "Oh, Zack!" she said. "You're coming to my auntie and uncle's with me this afternoon, aren't you?"

"Yep," said Zack, slinging his shoe bag over his shoulder. "And I'm starving! What's for lunch?"

"Whatever it is, it'll be fab-u-*lous*," said Poppy happily.

Her Uncle Simon, who owned a restaurant called Forrester's, had trained as a chef. What he made was always a surprise, and always delicious.

"I can't wait to meet Lucky, too," said Zack as they waited in the doorway. "This is going to be a fun afternoon!"

Lucky was Poppy's new puppy. Although he belonged to her, he lived at Auntie Jill's house because it had a big garden for him to explore. He was, Poppy often thought, a very lucky dog!

A silver car drew up, and Uncle Simon put

his head out of the window. "Hop in, kids,"
he said. "Lucky's in the back. We've just been
for a walk on the seafront."

Lucky barked, and Poppy and Uncle Simon
laughed. "He's saying hello!" said Poppy.

All the way home Lucky kept "talking"
to Poppy and Zack. "He's great!" said Zack,
which made Poppy feel very proud of her
puppy. As soon as they got to Uncle Simon
and Auntie Jill's house, Lucky and the
children rushed into the garden.

"Here, catch!" called Auntie Jill
from the kitchen door. She
threw Lucky's favourite ball,
a green one that he
liked to chase,
but also liked
to chew.

Zack caught it. "Fielded like a cricketer!" called Uncle Simon, tying on his striped apron.

Zack threw the ball for Lucky, who scampered across the lawn so fast his legs almost got tangled up. He picked up the ball in his mouth and bounded back to Poppy and Zack, dropping it at their feet and dashing round in circles, barking at the top of his voice.

"He's really enjoying himself," said Poppy. "He likes playing with you, Zack."

"And I like playing with him," said Zack, throwing the ball again. "Come on, Lucky, race you!" He ran off, with Lucky rushing round and round at his feet, leaping up and barking excitedly.

Poppy was happy to

watch Zack playing with the puppy. Unlike Zack, she saw Lucky almost every day. "Lucky's faster than you!" she called to him.

Lucky had got the ball and was dancing round Zack, waiting for him to throw it again. But as Zack got ready to throw the ball he took a step backwards, and Lucky was in the way. Zack's foot came down on Lucky's back, Lucky yelped, Zack lost his balance as he tried not to hurt Lucky, and the two of them ended up in a heap on the grass. Poppy ran to help. Lucky scampered off, but to her dismay, Zack didn't get up. He was sitting on the lawn, staring at his left wrist. His face was white.

"What is it?" she asked. "Have you hurt yourself?"

"My wrist," said Zack in a small voice. "And I feel a bit peculiar."

Poppy ran into the house, followed by Lucky, who didn't know it wasn't a game any more. Uncle Simon was stirring something in a saucepan. "Zack's hurt!" cried Poppy.

Her uncle looked round in surprise, took the pan off the stove and followed Poppy out immediately. He knelt down beside Zack and looked at him carefully. "Did you fall on that wrist?" he asked him.

Zack nodded miserably. Poppy could see he was trying not to cry.

"How does it feel?" asked Uncle Simon.

"Sort of like a bad headache, but in my wrist," said Zack, and then he *did* start to cry. He was also shaking a bit, as if he was cold, though it was warm in the garden.

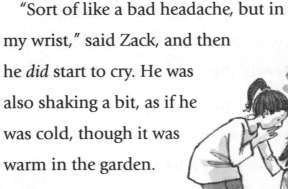

"Poppy," said Uncle Simon. "I'm going to take Zack to Accident and Emergency. Will you ask Auntie Jill to phone his mum and get her to meet us at the hospital?"

He lifted Zack off the grass. Zack looked like a rag doll in Uncle Simon's arms, his legs dangling and his left arm held awkwardly across his body. His wrist looked like it might be broken. Poppy felt like crying herself.

Auntie Jill came out to see what the fuss was about. When Uncle Simon explained, she took Poppy's hand. "Come on, hon," she said, "let's go and phone Zack's mum."

They watched Uncle Simon put Zack carefully into the car and do up his seat belt. As they drove away, Poppy couldn't hold the tears in any longer. "Oh, Auntie Jill!" she wailed. "I hope he'll be all right!"

"Try not to worry," said Auntie Jill, picking up the telephone to call Mrs Bishop.

"But … but…" Poppy was crying so much she couldn't speak. She sat down on the floor and put her hands over her face. It wasn't just that Zack had hurt himself and would need time to recover. It was that he wouldn't be able to dance properly with his arm in a plaster cast. The Nationwide Finals, as Miss Johnson had told them only that morning, were seven weeks away, and if Zack wasn't better by then...

Auntie Jill had finished speaking to Zack's mother. "What are you doing down here?" she asked Poppy, crouching beside her.

Poppy uncovered her face, which was all wet with tears. "How long does a broken wrist take to get better?" she asked.

"I don't know," replied her auntie. "A few weeks, I should think."

Poppy cried some more, then swallowed and sniffed. "Will he be better in time for Blackpool?" she asked.

Auntie Jill's face filled with sympathy. She put her arms around Poppy. "Oh, Poppy, I hope so!" she said.

Lucky had trotted in from the garden. When he saw Poppy crying, his tail went down. He nudged her gently with his nose, trying to lick the tears off her cheeks. Poppy held him close, feeling his little heart beating. She loved him so much, she couldn't bear to think that if Zack hadn't been playing with the puppy, he might not have got hurt.

"Poor Lucky," she said to him. "You don't know it, but today you've been Unlucky Lucky."

Lucky looked at her with his bright brown eyes. She kissed the top of his head. "Come on," she said, setting him down, "shall I throw the ball for you again?"

"That's right, Poppy," said Auntie Jill, getting up. "But you'll be careful, won't you? If you get hurt as well I don't know *what* will happen at Blackpool!"

Poppy and Lucky went into the garden. "Nothing's going to stop me and Zack dancing at Blackpool," she said to the puppy. "We *will* dance, I *know* we will!"

Irish Jive

When Zack arrived at class on Wednesday, everyone gathered round to inspect the plaster cast that reached from his knuckles to halfway up his left forearm.

"What happens if it gets wet?" asked Rosie.

"I don't know," said Zack. "They told me to keep it dry."

"So how do you have a shower?" asked Cora.

"He's got a special shower cap for it," Sam
told her. "With little ducks on!"

Zack laughed along with everybody else,
but Poppy could tell his eyes
weren't as bright as usual.

"Is it heavy?" asked Luke,
examining the cast.

"Not really," said Zack.
"But it's just … in the way.
Especially for dancing."

"As it's your left hand,"
said Miss Johnson, "you might want to use
the practice hold for a while."

Poppy knew this was sensible. Practice
hold was used when people didn't know a
dance very well, and had to concentrate on
their feet. Instead of taking each other in the
ballroom hold, where the boy had to hold

up the girl's right hand with his left hand at shoulder level, the partners just held each other's elbows. Practice hold would be more comfortable for him.

"No, it's all right, thanks," he said. "I want to dance properly, or not at all."

That's Zack! thought Poppy.

"Well, if you're sure…" said Miss Johnson doubtfully. "Let's warm up, then."

The children did stretches, running on the spot and lowering themselves in and out of invisible chairs. This was the most difficult exercise, and made their thighs hurt, but Miss Johnson said it made their legs strong.

Poppy glanced at Zack now and then during the warm-up. He kept his injured arm bent against his chest. The exercises were putting colour in his cheeks, though he still

looked glum. She hoped he'd be OK when
they started dancing.

"Ballroom first," said Miss Johnson.

The children had to know five ballroom
and five Latin dances for the Stardance
competition in Blackpool, though they
wouldn't find out until they stepped onto the
floor which ones they would have to perform.
Miss Johnson started the waltz music. Round
and round the studio went Poppy and Zack,
his right hand on her back, her left hand
on his arm, and his plastered hand
holding her right hand
up. The plaster, with
Zack's fingers coming out
of the end like sausages,
felt weird, but Poppy
tried to take no notice.

Then they did the foxtrot, a slow ballroom dance. Poppy could tell it was hard for Zack to hold the position of his arm, and when they launched into the next dance, the tango, it got harder. The striding, head-flicking tango was danced in the ballroom hold, but it also had a move where the dancers held their arms straight out instead of bending them at the elbow.

Zack dropped Poppy's hand. "I can't do this," he said to Miss Johnson. He was cradling his plaster cast in his other hand. "It hurts, and…"

He couldn't finish. His face looked creased up, like a beach-ball only half full of air. Miss Johnson put her arm round his shoulders. "Do you want to use practice hold?" she asked.

Zack shook his head.

"Why don't we *all* use practice hold, just for now?" suggested Sophie, looking worried.

Zack shook his head again. "What's the point?" he said sadly. "I might as well go home. I'm going to phone my mum."

He picked up his bag and left the studio. Poppy took a step to follow him, but Miss Johnson caught her hand. "Let him be," she said gently. "We'll think of something." She turned back to the class. "Now, Latin dances. Poppy, would you like to dance with me?"

When Poppy got home from school the next day, Auntie Jill was visiting with Lucky. The puppy jumped up all over Poppy as soon as she walked through the door. "Mind, Lucky!" she said. "Don't knock me over!"

She sat down on the sofa beside Auntie Jill. When Poppy had made enough fuss of Lucky, he settled down happily on her feet.

"How's Zack?" asked Auntie Jill.

"Fed up," said Poppy. "It's so unfair! He's refusing to come to classes until his plaster's off and he can dance properly, but that won't be until about a week before Blackpool, and he won't have done any practice. Even if I get through the first rounds, he might not, and I'll have to dance with someone else!"

Auntie Jill got up and put a DVD in the player. Poppy watched, wondering what her auntie was doing. She really didn't want to watch a movie now!

The DVD was of an Irish dancing show. The dancers performed intricate steps, in perfectly straight lines, with lots and lots of them on stage at once. Suddenly, Poppy knew what was in Auntie Jill's mind.

"They're not using their arms!" she cried.

"Exactly," said her aunt.

They watched the Irish dancers for a little while. Each one held their arms straight down at their sides while their feet flew so fast they were almost a blur. Poppy was amazed. "That looks impossible," she said.

"Listen, Poppy," said Auntie Jill. "Supposing you tried *ballroom* dancing with your arms at your sides? It would look strange, but what would it *feel* like?"

Poppy frowned, thinking. "You wouldn't be able to balance very well," she said. "You'd fall over."

Auntie Jill smiled. "So how do you think Irish dancers stop themselves from falling over?"

Poppy thought again. She tried to imagine dancing without using her arms. But she couldn't, so she got off the sofa. Lucky barked expectantly. Poppy went to the middle of the carpet, clamped her arms to her sides and did some jive steps. "Whoa!" she exclaimed as she almost fell against a chair. "This is *hard*!"

"Try again," encouraged Auntie Jill.

Poppy flicked her leg out from the knee while jumping

on the other foot in a basic jive step. It was a bit like the kicks in Irish dancing. She tried to keep her balance by using the muscles of her stomach and keeping her shoulders absolutely straight. She wobbled at first, but soon she found she could do it. "Look, Lucky," she cried. "The Irish jive!"

Auntie Jill laughed, and clicked off the DVD player. "It looks hilarious, but it's helped you strengthen your core muscles, hasn't it?" she said.

Poppy knew that all dancers must be strong in their core, which meant their middle, from their chest to the tops of their legs. She nodded. "I could feel my insides working," she said.

"So what do you think?" asked Auntie Jill.

"I think that if we all did our dances like

this for a couple of weeks, Zack wouldn't feel bad and we'd all get strong cores!" said Poppy. "*And* have a laugh as well!"

Auntie Jill got out her phone. "I'll get on to Sarah straight away," she said. Sarah was Miss Johnson. "And Zack's mum. Between us, we'll get Zack to class!"

"Sorry I'm late!" gasped Zack, hurrying into the studio. "My mum had to get petrol, and there was a huge queue."

"That's all right," said Miss Johnson. "Did she tell you what's happening today?"

"She said you wanted us all here, as we're starting something important," said Zack as he changed his shoes. "Otherwise I wouldn't have come, since I can't dance properly."

"How's your arm?" said Emma.

Zack looked down at his plaster cast, which looked grubbier than it had on Wednesday, and was covered with writing and drawing. "It's making my arm itch," he said. "And everyone in my class has had a go at it."

"You could put it in an art gallery and sell it for thousands of pounds," said Sam.

To Poppy's relief, Zack smiled. "Who'd get the money, though? Me or the kids that drew on it?"

"You would," said Cora, who had a tender heart. "Because it's your wrist that got hurt."

Zack nodded. But his smile had gone.

Miss Johnson started the warm-up music. When the children had finished their exercises, she stood in front of the class. "Someone's told me about a new technique," she announced, "and this morning I'd like to try it out. Copy what I do."

Poppy couldn't see Zack's face from where she stood, and she didn't dare look at anyone else in case she giggled. She kept her eyes on Miss Johnson, who was tracing the steps of the foxtrot, but with her arms held straight down at her sides.

Everyone copied her exactly. It looked weird, each child moving their legs but not their arms, gliding around in the slow, elegant dance like robots.

"Why are we doing this?" asked Poppy.

Really, of course, she knew.

"Wait and see," said Miss Johnson. "Let's try something faster."

She changed the music and started to do the bouncing step of the samba, rolling her hips but still not using her arms. All the children burst out laughing.

"That looks *mad*!" said Sophie as soon as she could speak.

"*Sad*, you mean!" said Luke.

"And *bad*!" added Emma.

"But quite 'armless!" said Sam.

"Just try it!" urged Miss Johnson, though she was laughing too.

Still giggling, the children began to do the "'armless" samba. They immediately found themselves staggering. Some of the children, including Poppy, spread their arms, trying to find their balance.

"Cheating!" called out Zack, whose arms had stayed down by his sides.

"You're really good at this, Zack," Rosie told him. "You must have brilliant balance."

"Especially since the plaster cast makes Zack heavier on one side than the other," said Miss Johnson. She had stopped dancing, and was walking between the children, watching as their balance improved. "Tell me what's happening to your stomachs," she said.

"Mine feels like it's got a tight bandage round it," said Cora.

"Good," said Miss Johnson. "That's your core muscles working. Dancing without arms is making you use those muscles, and we all know how important they are."

Gradually, the children became more serious. They couldn't laugh and concentrate on balancing at the same time. But to Poppy's delight, Zack's eyes were bright.

"How loony is *this*, Pop?"
he asked her as they did
a samba roll without
the arm movements.
A samba roll was where
the boy stood behind the
girl and they both rolled
their bodies, bending at their hips,
while doing the bouncing step round and
round. With no help from her arms, Poppy
could feel her tummy muscles working to
keep her body in the right position.

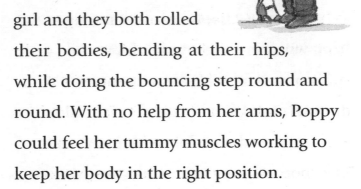

"Very loony," she said. "But it's fun, isn't it?"

The music changed again. "Everybody, do
the Irish jive!" called Miss Johnson.

"The *Irish jive?*" asked Zack, puzzled.
"What's that?"

"A jive with no arms," explained his teacher.

"In Irish dancing, they don't use their arms, but their feet flick, just like in the jive. Poppy'll show you."

Doing the jive with no arms was so funny the whole class ended up sitting, or lying, on the floor, laughing too much to go on.

"Well," said Miss Johnson, standing at the front with her hands on her hips and a wide smile on her face. "That was a success! What do you think about this idea? We could do every Wednesday class between now and Blackpool without using our arms. Maybe we'd get as good as Zack!"

Zack went a bit pink. Poppy suspected he knew that they'd planned this before he arrived, but he was pleased. He took her hand and helped her to her feet. "Anyone for the Irish tango?" he said.

Still laughing, the children stood up, clamped their arms to their sides and began to dance. As she and Zack strode round the floor, Poppy felt very happy. This was certainly the funniest dance class she'd ever done, thanks to Auntie Jill and the Irish jive. And best of all, Zack was back with her and their friends, doing what he liked best – dancing!

Poppy Goes for Gold

One week before the Nationwide Finals, Zack had his plaster cast taken off. Then the Easter holidays began, and it was time to leave for Blackpool.

Uncle Simon stayed behind to take care of Lucky and the Gemini Hotel for the weekend. Mum, Tom and Auntie Jill got into Dad's car, but Mrs Bishop offered to take Poppy with her and Zack. There was so much luggage that the boot of Dad's car wouldn't close. "Since we're all staying at the same hotel," said Mrs Bishop, "I can take some of your luggage as well."

"Besides Poppy, you mean?" teased Tom.

"Thanks, Trisha," said Dad to Mrs Bishop, hauling a suitcase out of the boot.

Poppy got into Mrs Bishop's car. "A piece of luggage isn't any trouble," she said, and made a face at her brother, who made a face back.

"Maybe it's a good job you two won't be in the same car," sighed Mum. It's a long way to Blackpool."

It *was* a long way. Poppy and Zack started off playing on his games console, and when Poppy was bored with that she did some puzzles in a magazine. After they'd stopped at a motorway service station Poppy fell asleep. She slept for a long time, but when she woke up, feeling very stiff, the motorway was still stretching ahead of them.

"It's about another hour," said Mrs Bishop.

"An *hour*?" repeated Zack. "Is Blackpool on another planet?"

Dusk was falling when they got there. As they turned on to the seafront, Poppy forgot all about being bored. People were walking by, chatting and eating ice creams. "Look!" exclaimed Poppy as a structure like a small version of the Eiffel Tower in Paris appeared ahead of them. "Blackpool Tower!"

Then she saw a pier, covered with lights and busy with people. And a few minutes later she saw another pier, equally crowded and brightly lit. Along the promenade there were displays of lights in different colours and designs. "Wow!" breathed Poppy. Then she saw yet *another* pier, and said, "Wow!" again.

"Look at that huge sandy beach!" exclaimed Zack.

"You can see why this is called the Golden Mile," said his mum. "A golden beach and bright lights too!"

"And a golden trophy, with any luck!" added Zack. He looked at Poppy excitedly. "We're ready to go for gold, aren't we, Pop?"

"YES in capital letters!" cried Poppy. "Gold ones!"

Mrs Bishop laughed. "There's your dad's car, Poppy," she said. "This must be the right hotel. And look, Lynn and Anna are already here, too."

Zack's Auntie Lynn and his cousin Anna, who used a wheelchair, had come from Birmingham to watch the Nationwide Finals, and were waiting in the hotel car park with the others. Poppy got out of the car and hugged Anna. "I'm so glad you're here!" she said.

"Thanks to you and Zack," said Anna's mum.

Poppy and Zack had come second in a local dance competition where the first prize was an all-expenses-paid trip to Blackpool. But the winner hadn't needed the prize, and had given it to Poppy and Zack so that Anna could come to see the dancing.

"It's great to see you again, Poppy," said Anna, smiling. "And you, Zack, and everybody!"

Dad lifted Poppy up and swung her round. "So what do you think of Blackpool?" he asked.

Perched in his arms, Poppy had a good view. "It's a bit like Brighton," she said, gazing at the promenade, the piers, the cliffs and the beach, "but bigger, and noisier, and more crowded, and … and…"

"And full of ballroom dancers!" finished Zack.

Mum was shaking Poppy gently. "Wake up," she was saying. "It's seven o'clock."

They didn't have to be at the Winter Gardens, where the competition was being held, until nine o'clock, but there was a lot to do first. Struggling to keep her eyes open, Poppy felt around on the bed for Lucky – not the real puppy but the soft toy she always took to dance competitions. She sat up. "Mum, where's Lucky?" she asked.

"Didn't you have him with you last night?" asked Mum.

"No," said Poppy, getting out of bed. "But I *must* have him with me today!"

"Don't worry," said Dad. "I'll look for him after breakfast while you're getting ready."

Neither Poppy nor Zack could eat anything. "Does your stomach feel weird too?" she asked him.

"Yep," he said. "Like I swallowed something too big for it. Maybe a shark." He sipped some water. "Or a crocodile."

Poppy had a very small glass of orange juice. By the time they went upstairs again, Poppy's heart had risen into her throat, and she couldn't breathe properly.

Auntie Jill had laid out Poppy's dance things on the bed, and Mum was setting out her make-up, hairbrush, hairpins, gel and spray on the dressing-table. Poppy and Zack had already had tanning lotion put on them at home. Zack had had his hair trimmed, and Poppy's fingernails had been painted pale pink. She sat down on the stool. In spite of her nerves, she was beginning to feel excited.

"Come on, Dad," said Tom, "we've got to find Lucky." He knew that taking Lucky to the competition was important to Poppy, just like him taking his football scarf to matches.

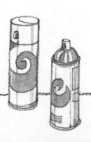

Through the mirror Poppy watched them opening and closing cupboards and cases. Tom checked the bathroom, and Dad searched under the furniture. They lifted clothes off chairs. They looked behind the net curtains. Tom even emptied his own bag. But Lucky was nowhere to be found.

"Poppy," said Mum, the eyeliner brush in her hand. "I can't do your eyes if you're all jittery."

Poppy tried to sit still, but her insides felt very jittery indeed. She'd taken Lucky to every competition, right from the very first one, and she and Zack *always* got through. If Lucky wasn't there, they might not.

Dad looked at Poppy seriously. "Are you quite sure you brought him?" he asked.

"Yes, I put him in my blue bag," said Poppy.

"What blue bag?" asked Tom.

Poppy's heart began to pound as Dad and Tom exchanged a dismayed look. "We must have left it at home in Brighton," said Tom.

Everyone was silent. Then Mum looked at her watch. "We'll have to leave for the ballroom in ten minutes," she said.

"But we can't go without Lucky!" blurted out Poppy.

Auntie Jill put her arm around Poppy's shoulders. "The rules say that if you're late they'll just go ahead without you," she said.

Poppy knew Auntie Jill, who had danced in important competitions herself, was right. She sighed. "Shall I put my dress on now?" she asked.

Her new Blackpool dress was so beautiful

it almost made up for the loss of Lucky. It was pale pink, and had a swirling skirt with a hem scalloped like the edge of a shell, showing the darker pink lining. On the bodice Mrs Heatherington, the dressmaker, had sewn sparkly pink beads, and she had made a sparkly pink hair decoration too.

Poppy stepped into the dress and Auntie Jill zipped it up. Then Mum fixed the decoration in Poppy's dark hair, which was pulled back into a tight bun and sprayed so that no strands would fall down when she danced. Poppy looked at herself in the long mirror.

"Oo-er!" said Tom.

Everyone laughed, but Poppy could see how proud they were. She felt grown-up and important, but a bit small and scared at the same time. Now she was dressed up like a princess, she just *had* to dance well, Lucky or no Lucky!

"We have to go," said Mum, putting a coat around Poppy's shoulders.

Zack, Anna, Mrs Bishop and Zack's auntie were waiting for them in the hotel lobby. Zack was dressed in black trousers, white shirt and black tie. His hair was shining and his eyes looked excited. "Ready?" he asked Poppy.

"Ready," she said. "But guess what – we can't find Lucky anywhere!"

Zack began to speak, but he didn't finish because Poppy's mum called to them, and they hurried out to the car park, where

Anna's mum was helping Dad put the folded wheelchair into his car boot.

"You're coming with me again, Poppy," said Mrs Bishop, opening the boot of her car to put Zack's dance bag in. "Oh!" she exclaimed. "What's this?"

Poppy peered in. There, almost hidden under some coats, was her blue bag. And sticking out of the corner was a furry brown ear. "Lucky!" she exclaimed. "We thought we'd lost you!"

She held the toy puppy on her lap all the way to the town centre. But when the car stopped outside the Winter Gardens and she, Zack and Auntie Jill got out, she almost dropped Lucky in amazement.

The Winter Gardens
weren't gardens at all, but a building
so large it went on and on down the street.
The lobby was full of children dressed for
dancing, with immaculate hair and shining
faces. Poppy saw so many different colours
she could hardly take it in. The whole scene
was like a carnival. No wonder the weekend
was called a dance *festival*!

"Look at this place!" gasped Zack, gazing
up at the ceiling as they emerged in a huge,
glass-covered room.

"This is still part of the lobby," Auntie Jill told them. She had competed at the Winter Gardens often during her career. "You wait till you see the ballroom!"

When the others arrived, a man at the door of the ballroom checked their tickets and motioned them through. Poppy tried to follow, but Auntie Jill pulled her arm gently. "You and Zack have to go to the green room," she said. "The first round's starting soon. But you can come and watch later, if you like."

"What green room?" asked Zack.

"It's not really green," said Auntie Jill. "But for some reason the place where performers wait is always called the green room. Miss Johnson's there already, I expect."

Poppy and Zack were hugged by everyone except Tom, who said "Yo!" and high-fived them. Poppy kissed Lucky and left him with Anna. Then they followed Auntie Jill to a room with a door on the other side that led to the Empress Ballroom. The music for the warm-up was beginning, but it was almost drowned out by the noise in the room. A hundred nervous children were crowding around the door to the ballroom with their teachers. The first round of the Stardance was about to begin.

The Stardance competition was especially for children of Poppy and Zack's age. As they passed the test in each dance, they were given a medal to put round the edge of their Stardance display board. When all twelve spaces on the board were filled, they got a gold star to put in the middle.

All the other Stardance competitors at Blackpool had that gold star. But to compete in Stardance at the Nationwide Finals, they had to have done well in their local Stardance competition. Poppy and Zack had done *very* well in theirs – they had come second, and won the silver shield.

The green room was cramped, and just as Poppy's aunt had said, wasn't green at all, but cream-coloured. "Oh, there's Miss Johnson!" said Zack. "And the others! Hello, everybody!"

Their teacher was looking very pretty in a black dance skirt and white top, with her hair in a French pleat and more make-up on than usual. Poppy was very pleased to see her, and all their friends from the dancing school. Emma had a black dress trimmed with gold.

Rosie was in silver, Cora's dress was red and Sophie's a soft yellow that set off her fair hair beautifully. "You look great!" said Poppy admiringly.

"So do you," said Emma. "Pretty in pink!"

When Auntie Jill had gone, Miss Johnson pinned numbers on the children's backs. Poppy's was 133 and Zack's was 351. "Ready for the warm-up, everyone?" she asked. "Girls, remember the judges are looking at you first, then it's the boys' turn."

Poppy and the other girls nodded. The judges only judged one partner at a time, except in special "couples" events. Because there were more girls than boys, each competing girl had to dance with someone who *wasn't* competing in the same event. Poppy, Sophie and Cora danced with Zack, Sam and Luke as usual, but Emma, who had no boy partner, danced with Miss Johnson, and Rosie danced with a girl called Debbie, who was competing in the events for older children.

When they entered the ballroom, Poppy gasped. She and her friends gazed in amazement at the spectacular Empress Ballroom. "It's like something in a fairy story!" said Rosie.

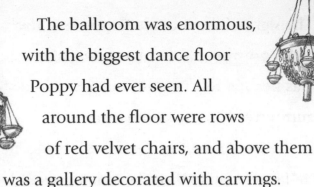

The ballroom was enormous, with the biggest dance floor Poppy had ever seen. All around the floor were rows of red velvet chairs, and above them was a gallery decorated with carvings. Columns supported a high, arched ceiling covered with beautifully painted panels, and chandeliers hung from long chains.

There were lights on the columns, too, and the dance floor was lit from above by stage lights. Along one side was a red-curtained stage, where the announcer and the person who controlled the music sat at little tables. The stage was decorated with flowers along the edge, and in front of the flowers stood the five judges.

The sight of them made Poppy's stomach tighten. She could hardly believe she was here, in this beautiful place, surrounded by the best dancers in the whole country.

"I can't wait to start dancing! "she said as she and Zack walked out onto the floor to join the warm-up.

Under the stage lighting the colours of the dancers' clothes glowed especially brightly, and their faces appeared so smooth they looked almost unreal, like faces in paintings or people on TV. Mum, Dad and the others waved, and Anna held up Lucky. Poppy waved back, smiling, though her stomach was suddenly full of butterflies, and her legs felt wobbly.

The warm-up music stopped. "Stardance Girls, First Round," said the man at the microphone.

"This is it, Pop," said Zack. "Let's do it."

Although the judges would be judging *her* this time, Poppy knew Zack would dance his best too. But so would the hundred children surrounding her. She knew she and Zack must dance better than they ever had in their lives to make it through to the next round.

"Samba and waltz," said the announcer, drawing the names of one Latin and one ballroom dance out of boxes. And before Poppy had time to catch her breath, the samba music started.

As soon as she started to move, her legs felt normal again. She and Zack samba'd round and round, trying not to collide with anyone else on the crowded floor. Poppy liked all the Latin dances, with their swaying, rolling movements and music that always sounded as if someone was having a party. But she *loved* the samba, the Brazilian carnival dance. You just couldn't help feeling happy when you were doing its bouncing, swishing steps, even in a competition!

The waltz had simple steps, but Poppy and Zack had practised for hours to get everything else right. Their arms, backs, shoulders, heads and hands had to be perfectly placed, and they had to remember to rise onto their toes and lower their feet again, all exactly in time to the music.

When it was over, Poppy and Zack hardly had time to draw breath before the boys' first round was announced. "Samba again, and quickstep," said the man.

Poppy and Zack smiled at each other. They knew they were good at the samba, so it was lucky that *both* of them were going to be judged on it. Poppy danced as well as she could, just like Zack had when the judges weren't marking him. In the quickstep, she knew that she and Zack's little running steps were *exactly* together, like they should be.

"Lovely!" said Miss Johnson to all her pupils when they came off the floor.

"I'm having the best time!" said Cora.

"Me too!" said several of the others.

"So was all that hard work worth it?" asked Miss Johnson, laughing.

"Yes!" they chorused.

They all got through to the next round, and the quarter-final. Poppy and Emma got through to the girls' semi-final. They felt sorry for Cora, Rosie and Sophie, but good-natured Sophie said, "It's OK. Not everyone can get through – that's the point!"

Poppy and Zack had a lot of space to move around in, as only twelve girls were left in the competition. The dances drawn for the girls were the jive and the foxtrot. Poppy liked doing the jive – especially when she could use her arms! She put all the energy she could into the kicking steps, the scalloped hem of her dress bouncing around her legs.

The foxtrot was a slow, elegant dance, so different from the jive it gave Poppy the chance to show off everything she could do. She tried very hard to make both the Latin and the ballroom dance look correct and well-placed, but natural, "as if you're part of the music," Miss Johnson always said.

Zack and Sam got through to the boys' semi-final, where the jive was drawn again. "Lucky's bringing us luck," said Poppy.

"Better luck than the real Lucky brought me!" replied Zack, holding up his left wrist.

Zack's ballroom dance was the Viennese waltz. As they turned and turned around the huge floor, Poppy felt as though she really was part of the lilting waltz music.

And Zack was doing the waltz so perfectly, they *must* put him through to the final.

The semi-finalists waited nervously in the green room, listening carefully as the names of the six girl finalists were announced. One, two, three, four places went to girls from other schools. Four families  screamed, and four girls were hugged by their teachers and friends. Then, after a short pause, the announcer said, "Number one-eight-two, Emma Feltham."

Emma put her hands over her mouth. "Oh!" she gasped.

Poppy was very happy for her friend, but before she could congratulate her, the next announcement came. "Number one-three-three, Poppy Love."

This time Miss Johnson put her hands over her mouth with a little shriek, and Poppy could hear shrieks from the ballroom too. As she and Zack ran out to be welcomed onto the floor, she saw the Blue Horizon Dance Studio supporters shouting and applauding louder than anyone else.

Emma, who was dancing
with Sam, looked as proud
as Poppy felt. Poppy forgot
all about losing Lucky, and
Zack had forgotten all about his
broken wrist. Both of them danced the
cha-cha-cha and the tango as if they could go
on for a thousand years and not get tired.

Zack was the only one of the boys to make
it through to the final. His face went pink,
then white, then pink again, and he pinched
his arm. "I *am* dreaming, aren't I?" he said.

The boys' dances were the samba and the
quickstep. "Lucky again!" said Zack
as they launched once more into
the Brazilian carnival dance.
And they did the quickstep,
which they'd had

some trouble with in the past, better than ever before. It *was* like a dream.

And a moment later, it got even more like a dream. When Poppy and Zack got back to the green room they saw another teacher, a tall woman with red hair, shaking Miss Johnson's hand. "Three finalists!" she said. "Well done!"

Miss Johnson went pink. "Thank you so much!" she said. "But the children did all the hard work."

"My name's Helen Ford," said the other teacher. "You're Sarah Johnson, from the Blue Horizon, aren't you? I teach at Burne Hall."

"Pleased to meet you," said Miss Johnson. "That's a full-time dance school, isn't it?"

Miss Ford nodded, and beckoned to a boy, who approached shyly. Poppy recognized

him. He had come third in the Juvenile Boys'
Ballroom event, for children slightly older
than the Stardance children. Like Zack, he
had brown eyes and brown hair that stuck up
a bit in front. And like Zack, he danced every
dance as if it was the most important thing
he'd ever done.

"I'd like you to meet Nick Price," said the
teacher. "He's one of my pupils. We teach
mainly ballet at Burne Hall, but our pupils
do other kinds of dance too. Nick's very good
at ballroom, but I can't find him a suitable
partner, at school or anywhere else."

"We've tried hundreds," said
Nick, smiling.

"Well, certainly
a lot anyway," said
his teacher.

"Anyway, we noticed Emma Feltham has no partner, and wondered if she would like to try out with Nick." She smiled at Emma. "You're one of the best dancers of your age I've seen," she told her. "We thought it was too good an opportunity to miss."

Poppy's heart began to thump. On special days like this, wishes *could* come true – couldn't they?

"That's a great idea!" exclaimed Miss Johnson. "Would you like to, Emma?"

Emma clasped her hands together in excitement. "Yes, please!" she said.

"Excellent," said Miss Ford. "After the results, you two can have a try-out."

The finalists lined up for the results. Poppy stood under the lights, smiling and listening to the applause. Her legs felt wobbly again,

though she
held the
position of
her feet as
steady as her
smile. "Come
on, Lucky," she said to herself,
"You know we danced well. Please, please…"

Sixth, fifth, fourth and third place went to
girls from other schools. Poppy could hardly
breathe. Then she heard the announcer say,
"Second, number one-eight-two, Emma
Feltham!"

As Emma went up onto the stage to
collect her trophy, Poppy saw Auntie Jill and
Emma's mum jumping up and down with
their arms around each other, and everyone
else clapping and stamping. There was

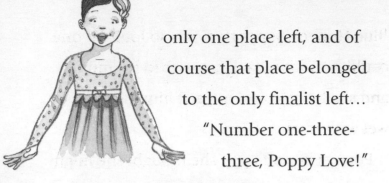

only one place left, and of course that place belonged to the only finalist left...

"Number one-three-three, Poppy Love!"

Poppy's legs really did feel as if the bones in them had disappeared. She held on tightly to Zack's hand as she took her applause. His mum was dabbing her eyes with a tissue, and Mum and Dad were leaning on each other, so overcome they had to prop each other up. Miss Johnson was being congratulated by everyone.

When the boys' results were read out, sixth, fifth, fourth, third and second place went to boys from other schools. The announcer tried to say, "First place, number three-five-one, Zack Bishop!" but the noise from the

Blue Horizon supporters was so loud no one could hear him. Zack ran over to his mum, and she hugged and hugged him, her cheeks wet with tears.

Poppy was so happy she thought she might burst. She and Zack had had lots of ups and downs on the way to these Finals, but it had all been worth it. The feeling of being the winner – the best Stardance dancers in the whole country – was so overwhelming she could hardly take it in. This was, she decided, absolutely the best day of her life.

"Are we good or *what?*" Zack asked her when they came off the stage with their trophies.

"We're brilliant!" Poppy replied.

They posed for photographs, and Poppy was hugged by lots of people, though she didn't know who some of them were. Anna and her mum were overjoyed. "We knew you could do it!" said Anna, waggling Lucky's paw.

"Hey, Poppy and Zack!" said Emma, appearing through the crowd with Nick at her side. "Meet my new partner! He's going to be coming to Miss Johnson's Saturday class."

"And you can come to Miss Ford's classes too," said Nick. "You're much better than all the girls at my school."

Emma looked at Poppy nervously. "Little Tom won't mind, will he?" she asked. "I usually dance with him in class."

"He'll be fine," said Poppy. "He's got loads of other girls to choose from!"

Emma looked relieved. "Today's been incredible, hasn't it?" she said.

"Totally," agreed Poppy. "I can't wait for next year."

"Will you still be dancing together next year?" Nick asked her and Zack.

Poppy and Zack exchanged a look. "Of course," said Zack. "We want to go on dancing together for ever."

"Maybe we'll be professional dancers, like my Auntie Jill," added Poppy.

"That's what *I'd* like to be," said Nick.

"Me too," said Emma.

Suddenly, Zack grabbed their right hands and put them in a pile on top of his own right hand. "Pact," he said solemnly. "In ten years' time, let's meet and do this again, when we're all professional dancers. Won't that be cool?"

All four of them raised their hands. In her other hand, Poppy still held the Stardance winning trophy. And in her heart, she knew they'd do it!

Natasha May loves dance of all kinds. When she was a little girl she dreamed of being a dancer, but also wanted to be a writer. "So writing about dancing is the best job in the world," she says. "And my daughter, who is a dancer, keeps me on my toes about the world of dance."

Shelagh McNicholas loves to draw people spinning around and dancing. Her passion began when her daughter, Molly, started baby ballet classes, "and as she perfected her dancing skills we would practise the jive, samba and quickstep all around the house!"